RETURN

LIBRARY OF DOOM

THE SEA OF LOST BOOKS

BY MICHAEL DAHL

ILLUSTRATED BY

www.raintreepublishers.co.uk
Visit our website to find out
more information about
Raintree books.

To order:
☎ Phone 0845 6044371
▤ Fax +44 (0) 1865 312263
▣ Email myorders@raintreepublishers.co.uk

Customers from outside the UK please telephone +44 1865 312262

Raintree is an imprint of Capstone Global Library Limited, a company
incorporated in England and Wales having its registered office at 7 Pilgrim
Street, London, EC4V 6LB – Registered company number: 6695582

Text © Stone Arch Books 2011
First published in the United Kingdom in hardback and paperback by
Capstone Global Library Ltd in 2011
The moral rights of the proprietor have been asserted.

Art Director: Kay Fraser
Graphic Designer: Hilary Wacholz
Production Specialist: Michelle Biedscheid
Originated by Capstone Global Library Ltd
Printed in and bound in China by Leo Paper Products Ltd

ISBN 978 1 406 22502 0 (hardback)
15 14 13 12 11
10 9 8 7 6 5 4 3 2 1

ISBN 978 1 406 22509 9 (paperback)
15 14 13 12 11
10 9 8 7 6 5 4 3 2 1

British Library Cataloguing in Publication Data
A full catalogue record for this book is available from the British Library.

Contents

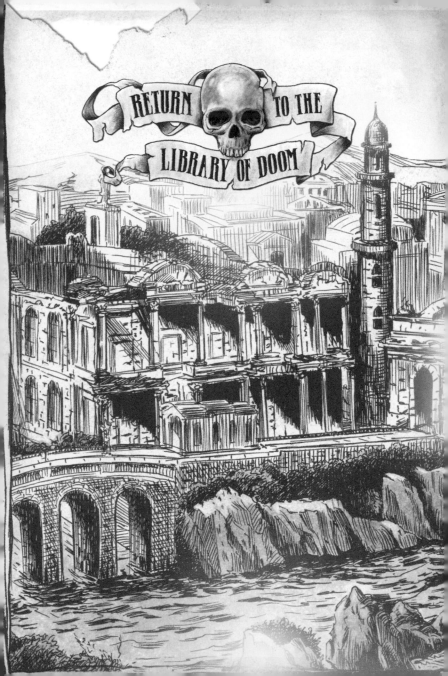

Behold the Library of Doom! The world's largest collection of deadly and dangerous books. Only the Librarian can prevent these books from falling into the hands of those who would use them for evil.

BUT WHAT HAPPENS WHEN THE LIBRARIAN HIMSELF FALLS INTO THE HANDS OF EVIL?

Chapter 1

THE SUNKEN ROOMS

At the edge of the Library of Doom, a dark sea roars.

Part of the library is built beneath

the WAVES.

Underwater rooms HOLD shelves

of books.

The books are made of jewels,

coral, and pearls. *

*

Sharks guard the watery rooms of the library.

They prowl between the shelves of books. They patrol the **SILENT** rooms.

Their mouths are full of razor-sharp **TEETH**.

A light **glows**.

The sharks stop swimming.

Their eyes fill with **fear**.

A shadow glides through the sea.

The sharks **FLEE**.

The shape moves towards the underwater rooms.

Long arms STRETCH through the water.

Each arm is full of poison.

The arms reach out towards the library.

Chapter 2

FLOATING TREASURE

The arms **WRAP** around the library's windows and towers.

Then the arms tighten.

They SQUEEZE hard.

The library rooms are **crushed**.

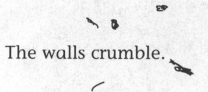

The walls crumble.

Books stream through the cracks.

They rush out like shoals of **frightened** fish.

The books **float** higher. Soon, they reach the surface of the sea.

They lie on the waves like flat, square islands.

The *shadow* moves beneath the floating books.

Glowing arms reach into the air. The arms belong to a **monstrous** jellyfish.

A huge air bubble floats at the centre of the **JELLYFISH**.

Inside the bubble stands a GIGANTIC man.

Chapter 3

ATLAS

The bubble rises higher. It RIDES on the waves.

The giant steps out of the bubble. He **steps** on to the floating books.

His body is covered with tattoos.

Each tattoo is a <u>letter</u>.

Across the back of his neck, tattoos spell his name.

His name is ATLAS.

Years ago, Atlas tried to destroy the LIBRARY OF DOOM.

But the Librarian defeated him.

Then he was **buried** alive, deep inside the Earth.

He planned his escape for years.

Now, the giant is **free**.

He stares into the SKY.

He is searching for someone.

Atlas spies a tiny shape.

It is flying in the distance.

"YES!" says Atlas. "I knew he would come!"

The shape grows larger.

It **SWOOPS** above the waves.

It is the Librarian.

The Librarian hovers above the **WAVES**. He points at the giant.

"You'll wish you'd never escaped from your prison, Atlas!" he cries.

Atlas scowls. "You'll never send me back!" he shouts.

The giant presses a finger against one of his **tattoos**.

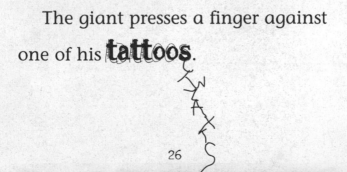

It is a letter. O.

The O flies off the giant's skin.

The O **SPINS**. It hums. It shoots through the sky.

It rushes towards the Librarian's head.

Chapter 4

DEADLY LETTERS

The Librarian snaps his fingers.

He **SPREADS** his hands apart.

The O starts to grow.

Soon, the Librarian can **pass** through it.

Then the letter turns into **SMOKE**.

It fades into the air.

"There's more where that came from!" cries Atlas.

He presses another letter on his arm. A giant **X** flies at the Librarian.

The X is a **MAGNET**. It pulls the Librarian on to its arms.

The Librarian cannot move.

The giant **jellyfish** glides towards the X. Long arms reach towards the Librarian.

"**One drop** of their poison, and you will be the Ex-Librarian," says Atlas.

The Librarian **CLOSES** his eyes. His glasses begin to shine.

Soon, his whole body **burns**
brightly.

Flames burst from the Librarian.

The X **breaks**.

The jellyfish is blinded.

It flees to the bottom of the **OCEAN**.

The Librarian is free.

He **flies** towards Atlas.

Chapter 5

FINAL PAPER

"Return these **BOOKS** to shore!" orders the Librarian.

"No. I don't care about them," says Atlas. "It is you I am after!"

A **LARGE** book floats beneath the Librarian.

Its covers slowly open.

The pages are wet.

The seawater has made them
SOGGY.

The Librarian cries out. He **falls**
from the air.

He lands on the wet pages of the
open book.

"I had many **YEARS** to think and plan," says Atlas.

"I learned everything I could about you and your Library. That's how I learned about your **WEAKNESS**."

"Wet paper," says the Librarian.

"You are **powerless** against it," says Atlas.

The Librarian sinks deeper. He is stuck in the slimy pages.

"Perhaps you need more C water," says Atlas.

He touches another tattoo.

The letter C leaps from his chest. It hangs above the Librarian's book.

The giant laughs. The C turns into water.

INKY rain spills on to the pages.

The Librarian cannot pull himself out of the black goo.

"Soon it will be all over," says the giant. "This is your last chapter. That book will be your GRAVE!"

The Librarian SINKS up to his chin.

WAVES splash on to the book.

The pages grow wetter and wetter.

Soon he will be **buried** in the paper.

Chapter 6

ENTER, SKYWRITER

Behind Atlas's head, another tiny shape flies in the distance.

The shape GROWS larger.

It **soars** above the waves.

The giant shouts, "How does it feel
to be buried **ALIVE?**"

The Librarian's hand sticks out
from the paper.

His **fingers** move weakly.

Suddenly, someone **swoops** down

and grabs the Librarian's hand.

He is pulled out of the book.

The Librarian looks **UP** at his

rescuer.

"Skywriter!" cries the Librarian. "I thought you were just a **LEGEND**."

Skywriter smiles.

"Let's find out how **real** I am," she says.

"Skywriter?" yells Atlas. "I will use your own **letter** against you!"

He touches an "S" tattoo on his arm.

The letter S grows into a **WHIP**.

The giant aims the whip at the woman. It wraps around her waist.

"Ah!" cries Skywriter.

She pulls the S whip off her waist.

Then she throws the letter back at the giant.

"Return to sender!" she says.

"NO!" screams Atlas.

The letter S wraps around Atlas's body.

Suddenly, he **SINKS** into the sea.

The Librarian turns to the **mysterious** woman.

"So the legend of Skywriter is true," says the Librarian.

The woman **NODS**.

"You protect the Books of Doom," she says. "I **PROTECT** the protector. You."

The Librarian looks around. He sees the floating books.

"I must **return** these books," he says.

"We'll need some help," says

Skywriter.

She **CLAPS** her hands together.

The **SOUND** travels through the sea.

A group of sea turtles paddle to the surface.

"Hardbacks" says Skywriter.
"They'll **FOLLOW** us."

The Librarian and Skywriter fly to
the Library.

Below them, the hardbacks — — — —
—> **PUSH** the books back to shore.

AUTHOR

Michael Dahl is the author of more than 200 books for children and young adults. He has won the AEP Distinguished Achievement Award three times for his non-fiction. His Finnegan Zwake mystery series was shortlisted twice by the Anthony and Agatha awards. He has also written the Library of Doom series. He is a featured speaker at conferences on graphic novels and high-interest books for boys.

ILLUSTRATOR

Bradford Kendall has enjoyed drawing for as long as he can remember. As a boy, he loved to read comic books and watch old monster movies. He graduated from university with a BFA in Illustration. He has owned his own commercial art business since 1983, and lives with his wife, Leigh, and their two children, Lily and Stephen. They also have a cat named Hansel and a dog named Gretel.

GLOSSARY

defeated beaten

destroy ruin completely

gigantic huge or enormous

guard protect from attack

hovers remains in one place in the air

legend story handed down from earlier times

monstrous horrible or scary

mysterious very hard to explain or understand

patrol guard an area

pressure force produced by pressing on something

rescuer person who saves another

terror very great fear

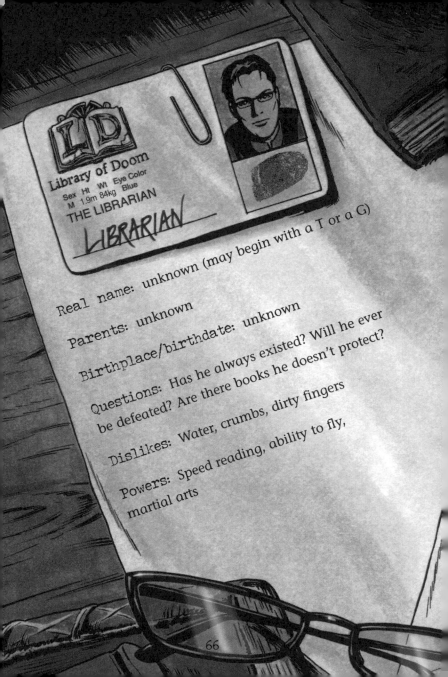

Library of Doom

Sex Ht Wt Eye Color
M 1.9m 84kg Blue
THE LIBRARIAN

LIBRARIAN

Real name: unknown (may begin with a T or a G)

Parents: unknown

Birthplace/birthdate: unknown

Questions: Has he always existed? Will he ever be defeated? Are there books he doesn't protect?

Dislikes: Water, crumbs, dirty fingers

Powers: Speed reading, ability to fly, martial arts

Library of Doom

Sex Ht Wt Eye Color
F 1.7m 68kg Brown

THE SKYWRITER

Skywriter

Real name: Sophia (last name unknown)

Parents: unknown

Birthplace/birthdate: United Kingdom, 20th century

Questions: What is her role in protecting the Librarian? Can she be stopped?

Dislikes: Bad listeners

Powers: Ability to fly, does not need sleep, can research anything, good handwriting

In Greek mythology, Atlas was a god who carried the world on his back. But in the world of the Library of Doom, Atlas is a terrible villain.

With letters tattooed on every inch of his body, Atlas might seem to be someone who loves words. But he's not. He is a thief of words. When the Librarian finally imprisoned Atlas decades ago, he thought that the world was safe. But Atlas used some of his tattooed letters to form a key, and was able to escape.

Atlas is now back in the dungeons of the Library of Doom, surrounded by armed guards. The Librarian has hired tattoo artists to try to erase Atlas's tattoos — before it is too late.

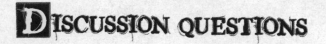

DISCUSSION QUESTIONS

1. Why did Atlas want to TRAP the Librarian?

2. What did you think about the title of this book? Does it match what you felt when you read the STORY? Can you think of any other titles that would be a good fit for this book?

3. Who do you think the Librarian is? Who is Skywriter?

WRITING PROMPTS

1. Make a list of five letters that are **TATTOOED** on Atlas's body in this book. (Don't use letters that were mentioned in the story.) What does each tattoo do?

2. Part of the Library of Doom is underwater. What kinds of books do you think are stored there? What are they about? Make a list of titles of books that might be kept in the underwater part of the Library.

3. **CREATE** a cover for a book. It can be this book or another book you like, or a made-up book. Don't forget to write the information on the back, and include the author and illustrator names!

More books from the Library of Doom

Attack of the Paper Bats
The Beast Beneath the Stairs
The Book that Dripped Blood
Cave of the Bookworms
The Creeping Bookends
Escape from the Pop-up Prison
The Eye in the Graveyard
The Golden Book of Death
Poison Pages
The Smashing Scroll
The Twister Trap
The Word Eater